# This First Christmas Night

**LAURA GODWIN**

*illustrated by* **WILLIAM LOW**

FEIWEL AND FRIENDS
NEW YORK

A FEIWEL AND FRIENDS BOOK
An Imprint of Macmillan
THIS FIRST CHRISTMAS NIGHT. Text copyright © 2016 by Laura Godwin.
Illustrations copyright © 2016 by William Low.
All rights reserved. Printed in China by Toppan Leefung Printing Ltd.,
Dongguan City, Guangdong Province. For information,
address Feiwel and Friends, 175 Fifth Avenue, New York, N.Y. 10010.

Our books may be purchased in bulk for promotional, educational, or business use.
Please contact your local bookseller or the Macmillan Corporate and Premium Sales Department
at (800) 221-7945 ext. 5442 or by e-mail at MacmillanSpecialMarkets@macmillan.com.

Library of Congress Cataloging-in-Publication Data
Names: Godwin, Laura. | Low, William, illustrator.
Title: This first Christmas night / Laura Godwin ; illustrated by William Low.
Description: First [edition]. | New York : Feiwel & Friends, 2016. | "A Feiwel and Friends book."
Identifiers: LCCN 2015034642 | ISBN 9781250081025 (hardcover)
Subjects: LCSH: Jesus Christ—Nativity—Juvenile literature. | Christmas—Juvenile literature.
Classification: LCC BV45 .G626 2016 | DDC 232.92—dc23
LC record available at http://lccn.loc.gov/2015034642

Book design by Patrick Collins
Feiwel and Friends logo designed by Filomena Tuosto

First Edition—2016
The artwork was created using Adobe Photoshop and Adobe Illustrator.

10  9  8  7  6  5  4  3  2  1

mackids.com

*This one is for Neil*
*—L. G.*


*For Anna and Stephanie,*
*with special thanks to Allen Shin*
*—W. L.*

See this small gray donkey,
this long, dusty road,
this promising star.

See this man, Joseph,
this woman, Mary.
Feel the frost on
this clear Bethlehem night.

See this inn with no room.

This humble stable, beckoning.
This simple manger with the smell
of sweet hay.

See these three wise men,
these camels,
these uncertain shepherds,
these soft, woolly sheep.

Hear the cattle lowing,

the doves cooing,

the lamb bleating,

the mother sighing.

Hear these angels singing.

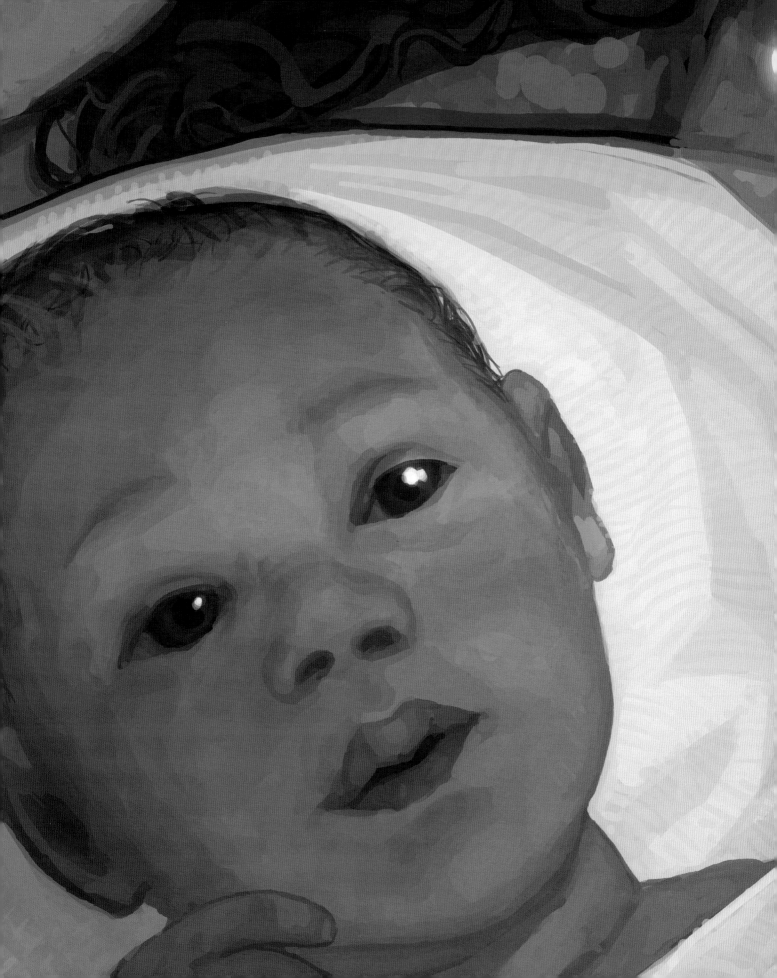

Welcome this tiny baby boy.

Feel this hush.

This peace on Earth.

This first Christmas night.